THOR

ATTACK ON ASGARD

Adapted by Elizabeth Rudnick

Based on the screenplay by Ashley Edward Miller & Zack Stentz and Don Payne

Story by J. Michael Straczynski and Mark Protosevich

NEW YORK

Published by Marvel Press, an imprint of Disney Publishing Worldwide. No part of this book may
be reproduced or transmitted in any form or by any means, electronic or mechanical, including
photocopying, recording, or by any information storage and retrieval system, without written
permission from the publisher. For information address
Marvel Press, 114 Fifth Avenue, New York, New York 10011-5690.

Printed in the United States of America

First Edition

1 3 5 7 9 10 8 6 4 2

J689-1817-1-11046

ISBN 978-1-4231-4636-0

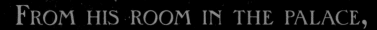

FROM HIS ROOM IN THE PALACE,
Odin Allfather looked out over the gleaming
kingdom of Asgard. He was troubled.
Today, his son Thor would become king.

"Do you think he's ready?" Odin asked
his wife, Frigga.

Frigga smiled. "He has his father's
wisdom," she answered.

Odin did not feel better. Sensing her husband's worry, Frigga added, "Thor will not be alone. Loki will be at his side to give him counsel. Have faith in your sons."

Odin sighed. He hoped she was right.

"Nervous, brother?" Loki asked when Thor joined him.

Thor's eyes narrowed. He knew Loki was teasing him. Loki liked to do that; he was the trickster in the family. Loki nodded at a goblet in the hand of a servant. Suddenly, it turned into writhing eels. The servant screamed and dropped the cup. Loki smirked.

"How do I look?" Thor asked, ignoring his brother and adjusting his long red cape.

"Like a king," Loki answered.

A horn sounded. It was almost time.

Loki left to take his place in the throne room. The huge space would soon be filled with the most respected men and women of Asgard.

Thor waited just outside. In moments, he would become king. While he would never dare admit it to his brother, Thor, he already he felt the pressure of the throne. He knew his father expected great things from him.

Thor heard footsteps behind him and turned. His mother was approaching. As always, she looked calm and regal.

"Thor," she said, smiling, "just remember that you have something the great Allfather never had."

Thor raised an eyebrow. "What is that?"

"Me for a mother." Then with a quick hug, she left.

As Odin began the ceremony, deep beneath the palace, guards stood watch outside the Vault.

The Vault was where Asgard's greatest threats were kept.

Suddenly, a cold breeze blew through the room. The guards shivered. Something was not right.

The guards walked to the end of the Vault. On a high pedestal sat the Casket of Ancient Winters. This was the most dangerous item in the Vault.

Just then, shadows fell over the casket. Looking up, the guards shouted.

The coldhearted Frost Giants had broken into the Vault!

Back upstairs, everyone had gathered in the throne room. They waited for the mighty Thor to arrive.

Loki stood at the front. Beside him were the Warriors Three—Volstagg, Fandral, and Hogun—and Lady Sif. These were Thor's closest friends. Odin sat on the throne. He did not look happy.

"Where is he?" Volstagg whispered.

"I wouldn't worry," Loki said. "Father will forgive him. He always does."

As if on cue, Thor entered the room.
There he stood, the greatest warrior
Asgard had ever seen. Thor raised his
mighty hammer, Mjolnir, high above his
head. The crowd cheered. Loki sighed.
His brother was always showing off.

Smiling, Thor knelt in front of his father.

"Today, I entrust you with the sacred throne of Asgard. Responsibility. Duty. Honor. They are essential to every soldier . . . and every king."

As Odin spoke, a chill ran through the room.

Then, as everyone watched, the large banners hanging from the ceiling began to freeze over.

Odin knew this chill all too well. The ancient enemies of Asgard were here!

Thor rushed out of the room. Loki, the Warriors Three, and Sif followed. When they arrived at the Vault, they saw the remains of a great battle. Blue-skinned monsters and Asgardian guards lay on the floor, lifeless. The Frost Giants had come for what they felt was rightfully theirs: the Casket of Ancient Winters.

Odin entered the Vault. His heart grew heavy as he took in the damage.

"The Frost Giants must pay for what they've done!" Thor shouted.

Odin saw the anger—and thirst for revenge—in his son's eyes. He sighed.

"I have a truce with Laufey," Odin said, referring to the Frost Giants' king. "What action would you take?"

"March into Jotunheim as you once did and teach them a lesson!" Thor answered with confidence.

But Odin would not hear of it. He was still king, and as king, he forbid his son to act. Jotunheim was to be left alone.

Later, in the banquet room, Thor paced
back and forth, fuming. Loki stood to the
side. This should have been Thor's day of
triumph. Instead, he was scolded like a
little boy.

Glancing at a long table filled with
delicious food and drink, Thor's anger
grew. He couldn't stand around and let the
Frost Giants get away with the invasion.
With a cry of rage, Thor flipped over the
banquet table, sending food and drink
flying.

"Redecorating, are we?" asked Lady
Sif, as she and the Warriors Three
entered the room.

"There's nothing we can do without defying Father," Loki said, trying to calm Thor.

Thor turned to his brother, a gleam in his eye.

"We are going to Jotunheim."

The others exchanged worried looks. This was madness. Thor was defying his father's direct orders! But they had no choice. They couldn't let Thor march into an enemy kingdom alone.

The next day, the group rode across the Rainbow Bridge. The bridge would bring them to Heimdall's Observatory. From there, they would take the Bifrost to Jotunheim.

When they arrived, the keeper of the Bifrost was waiting. Heimdall looked right through them with striking, almost unnaturally bright orange eyes.

"All is ready," Heimdall said. "You may pass."

Walking over, he inserted his sword into the Bifrost controls in the middle of the room. This controlled the Bifrost energy. The energy filled the room and then shot into space, creating a portal to Jotunheim.

Thor took a deep breath. There was no turning back now.

They were on their way to Jotunheim.

For Asgard. For revenge.